DEAR MR. HENSHAW

by
Beverly Cleary

Teacher Guide

Written by
Monica L. Odle

> ### Note
> The 2000 HarperTrophy paperback edition of the book, © 1983 by Beverly Cleary, was used to prepare this guide. The page references may differ in other editions. ISBN: 978-0-380-70958-8
>
> **Please note:** Please assess the appropriateness of this book for the age level and maturity of your students prior to reading and discussing it with them.

ISBN 978-1-56137-257-7

Copyright infringement is a violation of Federal Law.

© 2013 by Novel Units, Inc., Bulverde, Texas. All rights reserved. No part of this publication may be reproduced, translated, stored in a retrieval system, or transmitted in any way or by any means (electronic, mechanical, photocopying, recording, or otherwise) without prior written permission from ECS Learning Systems, Inc.

Photocopying of student worksheets by a classroom teacher at a non-profit school who has purchased this publication for his/her own class is permissible. Reproduction of any part of this publication for an entire school or for a school system, by for-profit institutions and tutoring centers, or for commercial sale is strictly prohibited.

Novel Units is a registered trademark of ECS Learning Systems, Inc. Printed in the United States of America.

ECS Learning Systems, Inc. recommends that the purchaser/user of this publication preview and use his/her own judgment when selecting lessons and activities. Please assess the appropriateness of the content and activities according to grade level and maturity of your students. The responsibility to adhere to safety standards and best professional practices is the duty of the teachers, students, and/or others who use the content of this publication. ECS Learning Systems is not responsible for any damage, to property or person, that results from the performance of the activities in this publication.

To order, contact your local school supply store, or—

Novel Units, Inc.
P.O. Box 97
Bulverde, TX 78163-0097

Web site: novelunits.com

Table of Contents

Summary 3

About the Author 3

Characters 4

Initiating Activities 4

Vocabulary Activities 5

Six Sections 6
   Each section contains: Summary, Vocabulary,
   Discussion Questions, and Supplementary Activities

Post-reading Discussion Questions 16

Post-reading Extension Activities 18

Assessment 19

Scoring Rubric 28

Skills and Strategies

Critical Thinking
Brainstorming, compare/contrast, inferences, evaluation, predicting

Comprehension
Cause/effect, drawing conclusions, decision-making, summarizing, creative thinking, identifying attributes

Writing
Poetry, short story, essay

Listening/Speaking
Discussion, dramatization, oral presentation

Vocabulary
Definitions, parts of speech, synonyms/antonyms, application

Literary Elements
Point of view, character analysis, figurative language, genre, theme, conflict/resolution, author's purpose

Across the Curriculum
Science—burglar alarms; Art—book cover, journal cover, postcard, sketch; Research—truck driving, Yellowstone National Park, Citizens' Band radios, butterfly gardens, famous author; Geography—locations on U.S. map

Genre: young-adult fiction

Setting: Pacific Grove, California

Point of View: first person

Themes: identity, family, friendship, love, forgiveness, resilience, positive thinking

Conflict: person vs. self, person vs. person

Style: informal, conversational

Tone: thoughtful, honest

Date of First Publication: 1983

Summary

In a series of letters and diary entries, Leigh Botts describes his struggle to cope with life since his parents' divorce. Leigh's father, a truck driver, communicates infrequently with Leigh. Leigh's mother, who works for a catering business, spends as much time as she can with her son but worries constantly about their expenses. During this lonely and difficult time, Leigh's main outlet for his feelings is his writing. At school, Leigh feels isolated and grows angry about repeated thefts from his lunchbag. Leigh's resentment toward his father deepens when he discovers that his father lost his dog, Bandit. However, certain adults in Leigh's life encourage him to think positively, and Leigh soon begins to mature. He makes friends, forgives his parents, and learns to respond to situations differently. By the end of the book, Leigh has made peace with his new reality.

About the Author

Beverly Cleary, a highly respected children's author, was born on April 12, 1916, in McMinnville, Oregon. Her small town had no library, so Cleary's mother created one. After moving to Portland, a young Cleary struggled to sustain interest in reading. Later, this motivated her to write books children wanted to read. Cleary attended Chaffey College, the University of California at Berkeley (where she received a B.A. in English), and the University of Washington. In 1940, she married Clarence Cleary, and the couple moved to California, where Cleary began writing. She recalled her mother's advice that "the best writing was simple and filled with humor" and advice from a professor to capture universal themes using details. Cleary's first book, *Henry Huggins*, was published in 1950. She has authored more than 30 titles, which have been published in many countries and in at least 14 different languages. Cleary is perhaps best known for her books about Ramona Quimby, written over a span of 44 years. *Ramona and Her Father* and *Ramona Quimby, Age 8* were named Newbery Honor books in 1978 and 1982, respectively. Cleary also received the Newbery Medal for *Dear Mr. Henshaw* in 1984. Her other achievements include the 1975 Laura Ingalls Wilder Award, the 1980 Regina Medal, and the University of Southern Mississippi's 1982 Silver Medallion. In 1984, the United States nominated Cleary for the Hans Christian Andersen Award. In 2000, she was named a "Living Legend" by the Library of Congress.

Characters

Leigh Marcus Botts: sixth-grade boy whose parents are divorced; struggles to cope with his dad's absence; writes to his favorite author about various goings-on in his life; wants to be a writer himself

Bonnie Botts: Leigh's mother; works for a catering business; takes nursing classes at a local college; supportive and caring

Bill Botts: Leigh's father; works as a truck driver; visits Leigh infrequently after the divorce; has trouble expressing himself; still in love with Leigh's mother

Boyd Henshaw: Leigh's favorite author; clever and sarcastic; gives Leigh advice in his response letters

Mr. Fridley: custodian at Leigh's school; gives Leigh the idea for a lunchbox burglar alarm; advises Leigh to think positively

Barry: boy in Leigh's grade at school; befriends Leigh after seeing his lunchbox alarm in action

Katy: owns a catering business; Leigh's mother's boss and friend; gives Leigh's mother special snacks to put in Leigh's lunch

Miss Neely: librarian at Leigh's school; encourages Leigh to submit a story for the Young Writers' Yearbook competition

Miss Martinez: Leigh's sixth-grade teacher

Angela Badger: famous author whom Leigh meets; praises Leigh's writing

Bandit: Leigh's dog; rides with Leigh's father on his truck routes

Initiating Activities

Use one or more of the following to introduce the book.

1. Brainstorming: Have students use the Attribute Web on page 20 of this guide to brainstorm about forgiveness. Ask students: What is forgiveness? How might forgiveness emerge as a theme in the book?

2. Research: Have students research truck driving as a profession. Ask students: How are truck drivers' jobs important to the economy? What are the job's challenges and rewards? Students should share their information and opinions with the class.

3. Discussion: As a class, discuss being new to a school, city, or other environment. Include in your discussion challenges a new person would face (such as making friends) and things other people could do to help someone new feel at home.

4. Point of View: Discuss the differences between third-person and first-person points of view. What predictions can you make about this book, which is written in first person (mostly in letter and diary form)?

5. Writing: This book deals largely with the main character's desire to understand and love his parents. Write a poem that describes a person's relationship with his/her parent or guardian.

Vocabulary Activities

1. **Sentence-by-Sentence:** As a class, brainstorm a sentence to start a story. Students should pass around one sheet of paper with the starter sentence at the top. Each student must add one sentence to the story. Each sentence must correctly use one vocabulary word from this guide. After each class member has contributed to the story, have a volunteer read the story aloud.

2. **Vocabulary Squares:** Select nine students to sit in three rows of three in the classroom. Give each student a large cut-out of an X and an O. Select two other students to compete. One student is "X," and the other is "O." Student X is asked to define a vocabulary word. S/he must choose one of the nine students sitting in a square to define the word, and then state whether s/he agrees or disagrees with the given definition. If Student X correctly agrees or disagrees with the given definition, the sitting student must display the X. If Student X incorrectly agrees or disagrees, the sitting student displays the O. Alternate turns between Students X and O. The first student to have three Xs or Os in a row (vertically, horizontally, or diagonally) is the winner.

3. **Vocabulary Mobile:** Have each student select a vocabulary word from the lists in this guide. Provide a coat hanger, string, and paper for each student. Each should create a visually intriguing mobile that clearly displays the vocabulary word, the word's definition, part of speech, synonyms or antonyms, and a visual representation of the word.

4. **Word Chain:** Divide the class into groups, and give each group the same set of 15 vocabulary words. The groups must write each word and its definition on a separate sheet of paper. Then, they must think creatively to connect the sheets together to form a chain. There must be a reason why each word is connected to the next. Reasons may be as varied as they both "start with j," "describe the main character," or "have to do with politics." Have students write the reasons at the bottom of each sheet as they connect them. The group with the longest chain is the winner. Display all word chains on a wall in the classroom.

5. **Start/Stop:** Divide the class into two teams. One person from each team will stand at one end of the room. Each team is given a vocabulary word at random, which the team must define without assistance. If that team can define the vocabulary word, its standing teammate may move forward one step and then stop. If the team answers incorrectly, the opposing team's standing member may move forward two steps. The team whose standing teammate reaches the opposite side of the room first wins.

May 12–November 16

Over a span of five years, Leigh Botts writes letters to his favorite author, Boyd Henshaw. After being disappointed by Mr. Henshaw's printed first letter, Leigh receives a handwritten letter that is more personalized. As a sixth grader, Leigh asks Mr. Henshaw to answer a list of questions for a book report. Mr. Henshaw answers Leigh's questions but also includes with his letter a list of questions for Leigh. This extra task angers Leigh, who refuses to complete it until his mother finds the letter and insists he write back to Mr. Henshaw.

Vocabulary

bulletin
diorama
mobile
enclosure
sincerely
mincemeat
autographed
urgent
argument
duplicated

Discussion Questions

1. Discuss the point of view from which *Dear Mr. Henshaw* is written. What are advantages and disadvantages of this point of view? *(The book is written from first-person point of view. Answers will vary. One advantage is that readers are able to view the world through the character's perspective, giving them a better understanding of the story. Disadvantages include often not knowing what other characters think or feel and having to rely upon the main character's impressions of others.)*

2. Identify two errors in Leigh's first letter to Mr. Henshaw. Why do you think he includes "boy" at the end of his name? *(Leigh misspells "liked" and "friend." Answers will vary, but students should consider that "Leigh" is used for both males and females or that Leigh's teacher asked students to identify their genders when writing to authors.)*

3. What does the reader learn about Leigh after his second letter to Mr. Henshaw? Why do you think Mr. Henshaw did not respond to Leigh's first letter? *(The reader learns that a year has passed and Leigh is now in third grade. The reader also learns that Leigh's reading skills have advanced, since he can now read* Ways to Amuse a Dog *on his own. The rest of the letter offers bits of information about Leigh's life. Answers will vary, but Mr. Henshaw may have been too busy to answer Leigh's first letter or perhaps he felt an answer wasn't expected of him.)*

4. What is humorous about Leigh's second letter to Mr. Henshaw? Discuss the significance of humor in a story. *(Leigh learns how to correctly spell "friend" but misspells "touch" at the end of his letter. Answers will vary. Humor is used to engage readers. The subtle humor Cleary uses adds dimension to the story. The letter becomes more than just a boy's musings to an author; it begins to reflect the personality of a maturing boy who is still learning but enjoys writing and sharing his experiences.)*

5. Describe Leigh's two fourth-grade letters to Mr. Henshaw. Why do you think Leigh continues to write to Mr. Henshaw, and what might Mr. Henshaw think of Leigh? *(Leigh expresses his continued interest in* Ways to Amuse a Dog *and requests that Mr. Henshaw send him a handwritten response letter. Leigh also reveals that he lives in a mobile home park and wants to be an author when he grows up. Answers will vary. Students might think Leigh continues to write to Mr. Henshaw because he is determined to get to know his favorite author better. He may also just like having someone to talk to.)*

6. What does Leigh's sixth-grade author report reveal about Mr. Henshaw? How does Leigh feel about Mr. Henshaw's letter? What lesson do you think Mr. Henshaw wants Leigh to learn from his response? *(Answers will vary, but Mr. Henshaw's humorous letter [which the reader does not have access to] reveals that Mr. Henshaw has a sense of humor and is mischievous. Though Leigh appreciates Mr. Henshaw's writing tips, he is annoyed that Mr. Henshaw included a list of*

questions for him, as this creates more work for Leigh. Answers will vary but might include that Mr. Henshaw is hinting that students should learn to use libraries and conduct research themselves, rather than placing that burden on someone else.)

7. What is the tone of Leigh's letter dated November 16? To what do you attribute his attitude? *(Answers will vary. Leigh's tone is intense and upset. He is irritated that his mother is insisting he answer Mr. Henshaw's questions. Students may also conclude that Leigh's anger stems from a difficult situation at home involving Leigh's father no longer living with the family.)*

8. **Prediction:** Where is Leigh's father?

Supplementary Activities

1. Character Analysis: Begin the Character Web on page 21 of this guide. Continue adding information as you read the book.

2. Art: Use information Leigh provides about the plot of *Ways to Amuse a Dog* to create a cover for that book.

November 20–December 21

Leigh begins to answer the questions on Mr. Henshaw's list. He reveals that his parents are divorced and that his dog, Bandit, stayed with his father, a cross-country truck driver. He also describes how he and his mother live in a small garden cottage near a gas station. Leigh tells Mr. Henshaw that he is new to his school, doesn't have many friends, and is frustrated because someone is constantly stealing items from his lunchbag. He also confesses that he misses his father and Bandit. Following Mr. Henshaw's suggestion, Leigh begins to keep a diary.

Vocabulary
apply
rotting
strudel
vocational
refinery
duplex
antique
cross
suspect
partition
composition

Discussion Questions

1. Why do you think Mr. Henshaw underlined the word "write" in his advice to Leigh? Why does Leigh's mom insist he respond to Mr. Henshaw, and what does this indicate about her character? *(Answers will vary. Mr. Henshaw likely emphasizes "write" to underscore its importance. Through his advice, Mr. Henshaw indicates that writing frequently is vital to becoming a professional author. Leigh's mom's insistence that he answer Mr. Henshaw's questions shows that she expects her son to be respectful and truly wants him to succeed. She also probably feels that writing is a good outlet for Leigh to express his feelings—an outlet he needs desperately due to his parents' recent divorce. This demonstrates that Leigh's mom cares for her son's well-being and future.)*

2. How does Leigh describe himself? Why do you think the author of the book presents Leigh in this light? *(Leigh describes himself as "plain" and "medium," explaining that he is not considered "Gifted and Talented" at school but is "not stupid either" [p. 15]. He instead refers to himself as "the mediumest boy in the class" [p. 15]. Answers will vary but should include that the author presents Leigh as ordinary to create a relatable character with universal traits.)*

3. What information presented thus far hints that Leigh's parents are divorced? *(Leigh moved to a new school for sixth grade and only ever mentions his mother's advice, rules, opinions, etc. after that. Leigh refers to his father in past tense, giving the impression that his dad is no longer around. Leigh also talks less about Bandit once he reaches sixth grade.)*

4. To what does Leigh attribute his parents' divorce? How does Leigh treat his parents after the divorce? *(Leigh believes his parents divorced because of his dad's insistence on owning his own rig. Leigh's mother thought that the down payment on the rig would have been better used to purchase a house, but Leigh's father disagreed. Leigh tries to be fair to both parents, as evidenced in his statement: "…I try to treat Mom and Dad the same…" [p. 17].)*

5. Why do you think Leigh describes his father's truck in such detail? What is Leigh's opinion of his father's occupation? *(Answers will vary. Perhaps Leigh provides such extensive detail because the truck represents the reason for his parents' divorce. Leigh also seems a bit wistful when describing the truck, demonstrating how he wishes for more interaction with his father. For Leigh, the truck is almost an extension of his father. Leigh may also admire the truck out of respect for his father, who treasures the rig. Leigh seems proud of his father's occupation.)*

6. How does Leigh help the reader envision the garden cottage where he and his mother live? Why do you think the author includes the illustration on pages 20 and 21? *(Leigh describes the ocean breezes and fog he and his mother experience, as well as nearby "golf courses for rich people" [p. 21]. He describes the cottage as "really little" and "falling apart." Leigh has his own room, and his mother sleeps on the living room couch. Near the cottage are a duplex, gas station, thrift shop, pet shop, sewing machine shop, electric shop, antique shops, and restaurants. Answers will vary but should include to show how close the cottage is to both the duplex and gas station.)*

7. How did Leigh's family acquire Bandit? Why is Leigh glad that Bandit rides with his father? What does this show about Leigh? *(Bandit jumped into Leigh's father's truck at a truck stop, and the family kept him. Though Leigh misses Bandit, he is glad Bandit is on the road having fun rather than alone indoors all day. Leigh also finds comfort in the fact that Bandit keeps his father awake during long hauls. Answers will vary, but Leigh seems logical, responsible, and considerate.)*

8. How does Leigh feel about school? Why? *(Leigh is not very enthusiastic about school. He says, "The best thing about sixth grade in my new school is that if I hang in, I'll get out" [p. 25]. Answers will vary, but Leigh's indifferent attitude about school likely stems from being ignored by classmates and not having any real friends. Leigh probably feels unimportant. He is also irritated that someone has been stealing from his lunchbag every day.)*

9. Why do you think Leigh lashes out as he finishes answering Mr. Henshaw's questions? *(Answers will vary. Some students may think Leigh is angry because he was forced to do extra work, but others may realize that there are underlying reasons for Leigh's anger—such as his parents' divorce, moving to a new town and school, and wishing to spend more time with his father.)*

10. Why does his morning "job" with Mr. Fridley make Leigh so happy? *(Having a reason to arrive at school early means Leigh doesn't have to walk to school slowly anymore. Subconsciously, Leigh is excited to be noticed at all. Helping Mr. Fridley makes Leigh feel useful and important.)*

11. Why do you think Mr. Henshaw suggests Leigh begin writing in a diary? Do you think Mr. Henshaw cares about Leigh? Why or why not? *(Answers will vary, but Mr. Henshaw most likely thinks Leigh needs an outlet for the stress he feels about family and school problems. As a professional author, Mr. Henshaw is not able to constantly communicate with Leigh. Mr. Henshaw probably also thinks the writing practice is a good idea for an aspiring writer. Though it seems Mr. Henshaw emphasizes that he is busy, he also continues to write to Leigh and offers him wise advice. This indicates some level of concern for Leigh on Mr. Henshaw's part.)*

12. **Prediction:** What will Leigh write about in his diary?

Supplementary Activities

1. Writing: Write a short story titled "The Great Lunchbag Mystery." Your short story may use Leigh's situation in its plot, or you may create an entirely new plot.
2. Art: Make a list of your favorite things (e.g., favorite food, favorite color, favorite type of pet). Use your list to create a digital or print collage that could serve as a personalized journal cover.
3. Critical Thinking: Think about an activity or place that helps you feel calm when you are under stress. Explain why your particular calming method works for you.

Friday, December 22–January 19

Leigh begins writing in his diary, and his first entry describes his frustration with the person stealing from his lunchbag. After anxiously awaiting a gift from his father, Leigh is extremely excited when a trucker drops off a package for Leigh on Christmas Eve. After temporarily solving his lunch problem by printing the name "Joe Kelly" on his lunchbag, Leigh is disappointed when part of his lunch is stolen again. Mr. Fridley suggests Leigh use a burglar alarm on his lunchbag. Leigh reads Mr. Henshaw's new book and considers entering a writing competition.

Vocabulary
foil
broiled
juke box
retainers
beggar
hibernated
relieved

Discussion Questions

1. Why doesn't Leigh report the thefts from his lunch? *(Leigh does not report the thefts because he believes "it isn't a good idea for a new boy in school to be a snitch" [p. 39]. Whether Leigh believes this because he has experienced it in the past or he just wants to be well-liked, he realizes "complaining" to the teacher isn't going to win him any friends.)*
2. How might one shoe lying on the highway be compared to Leigh's father? *(Answers will vary, but like the single shoe, Leigh's father is now divorced—or without a mate. Like the single shoe on an open road, Leigh's father is alone on his life's path as a result of the divorce.)*
3. Why does Christmas cause mixed feelings for Leigh? *(Initially, Leigh is disappointed that someone continues to steal from his lunch. However, he cheers himself up by planning a solution to this problem to try after Christmas break. Leigh waits anxiously for a gift or call from his father. He is saddened by memories of Christmas with both parents present. When a truck driver delivers a gift for Leigh, Leigh is ecstatic. He enjoys Christmas dinner at Katy's house, though it is not the same as having Christmas with his parents.)*
4. Describe the two methods Leigh employs to keep his lunch safe. What does Mr. Fridley suggest, and what does Leigh think of this idea? *(Leigh tries labeling his lunchbag "Joe Kelly" to deter the thief, but this solution only works temporarily. Then, Leigh secures his lunch with Scotch tape. This idea backfires when the tape prevents Leigh from being able to easily open his own lunch. Mr. Fridley suggests that Leigh get a burglar alarm for his lunch, which Leigh initially thinks is a silly idea. However, Leigh begins to seriously consider the idea after a time.)*

5. What does the conversation between Leigh and his mother reveal about each person? What does it reveal about their mother-son relationship? *(The conversation reveals that Leigh wishes for a father figure and does not understand [1] the real reason his mother and father divorced or [2] that marrying someone is complicated and requires much thought. It also reveals that Leigh's mother is intelligent, selective, and not in a hurry to date or get remarried. Lastly, the conversation reveals that Leigh and his mother communicate openly and honestly.)*

6. How is *Beggar Bears* different than the other books Leigh has read by Mr. Henshaw? Why do you think the book affects Leigh so deeply? *(Unlike Mr. Henshaw's other books, Beggar Bears is not humorous. Its subject matter is more mature and its plot more suspenseful, adopting an environmental angle. Answers will vary, but Leigh's musings about the mother and father bears suggest that he identifies with the orphaned baby bears. Like the baby bears, Leigh feels lonely and as if his family has been split apart. Leigh may also worry about what he would do if something happened to his mother.)*

7. How has Mr. Henshaw's advice to write continually affected Leigh's life? *(Leigh's teacher tells him his writing skills are improving. On a personal level, writing has helped Leigh cope with the strain of his parents' divorce and his loneliness. He tells Mr. Henshaw, "I think I feel better when I write in my diary" [p. 58]. Writing has also helped Leigh get noticed at school, as his teacher has suggested he submit a story for a writing competition.)*

8. **Prediction:** What will Leigh's story for the writing competition be about?

Supplementary Activities

1. Figurative Language: Illustrate the simile, "Katy has a heart as big as a football stadium" (p. 44).
2. Research/Writing: Research Yellowstone National Park. Prepare a brief report about when it was established, where it is located, and what types of animals can be found there.

Saturday, January 20–Monday, February 5

Leigh struggles to compose a story for the writing competition and becomes angry when his father breaks his promise to call. Confused, Leigh alternately blames himself and his parents for the divorce. He recalls a fun-filled truck ride he once took with his father. One night, when Leigh is home alone, he calls his father in Bakersfield. Leigh is infuriated to discover that his father has been home but has not called him and is further upset that his father lost Bandit and is apparently spending time with a woman and her son. When Leigh's mom arrives home from nursing class, she and Leigh have an honest conversation.

Discussion Questions

1. How do Mr. Fridley and Leigh's mother each respond to Leigh's anger toward his father? How does Leigh feel as a result? *(Mr. Fridley tells Leigh, "Don't think you are the only boy around here with a father who forgets" [p. 62]. Leigh's mother tries to explain how difficult a trucker's life can be. While both adults' advice makes Leigh consider others' situations [rather than feeling sorry for himself], Leigh is still angry with his father. He is lonely and struggles to believe his father loves him. He even begins to question whether he caused his parents' divorce.)*

Vocabulary
ulcers
alfalfa
wrath
civilization
legal
mildew
stranded
reception
blubbered
sagebrush
breakers

2. Why do you think Leigh remembers a particular truck ride with his father so vividly? *(Answers will vary, but Leigh likely remembers this ride fondly because of how important he felt riding with his father. Leigh's father introduced him to everyone at the truck stop, and the two ate heartily and played games together. Perhaps that particular trip was when Leigh felt most loved by his father. Now, when he is missing his father terribly, Leigh probably recalls this trip to make himself feel better.)*

3. What further upsets Leigh when he speaks to his father on the phone? What do you think upsets him most about this conversation, and why? *(Leigh finds out that his father lost Bandit during a snowstorm. He also overhears a boy's voice in the background, asking Leigh's father about dinner plans with the boy and his mother. Answers will vary, but students should recognize that Leigh hangs up the phone feeling replaced and unimportant. He also realizes his father had no intention of calling him that week.)*

4. Why does Leigh claim he cannot hate his father? *(Answers will vary. Although Leigh is furious and hurt, he can't deny that he still loves his father. It seems Leigh grasps the fact that he feels so deeply because of his love for his father. Leigh is simply bitter that his father is no longer a large part of his life [and perhaps jealous that another boy is receiving the attention Leigh so desperately craves].)*

5. How does a conversation with his mother help Leigh feel better? What do you learn about each character from this conversation? *(Talking with his mother helps Leigh understand his father better. His mother also says that, at a certain point in her life, she "had had enough of highways and truck stops" [p. 75], making Leigh realize he didn't ruin his parents' relationship when he was born. Leigh's mom even makes him feel better about Bandit, suggesting the dog simply moved on to another person's truck. From this conversation, the reader learns that Leigh is curious, understanding, and forgiving and that his mother is realistic but still loves Leigh's father.)*

6. Why does watching the ocean waves make Leigh's mother feel hopeful? *(The waves help reassure Leigh's mom that "no matter how bad things seem, life will still go on" [p. 78]. This reassurance is especially meaningful to Leigh and his mother at that moment, since each is struggling emotionally.)*

7. **Prediction:** How might Leigh's relationship with his father change from this point forward?

Supplementary Activities

1. Cause/Effect: Complete the Cause/Effect Chart on page 22 of this guide.
2. Research/Writing: Research how Citizens' Band radios work. What different professions use them, and why? Write a one-page essay with your findings. Include an illustration of a CB radio.

Tuesday, February 6–Saturday, March 17

Leigh's frustration mounts as he yearns for friends and a sense of normalcy. Observant Mr. Fridley notices Leigh's gloom and offers him advice. On his way home from school, Leigh visits a butterfly garden, which inspires renewed hope in him. He begins writing a story for the Young Writers' Yearbook. Needing an author's advice, Leigh writes to Mr. Henshaw about the problematic ending to his fiction story. Using money his father sent him, Leigh purchases hardware and carefully constructs a burglar alarm for his lunchbox. When no one steals anything from his lunch, Leigh must activate the alarm himself in the cafeteria. Barry befriends Leigh, whose burglar alarm idea spreads school-wide. Leigh finally speaks to his father on the telephone again.

Vocabulary
billions
positively
grove
flitting
villains
insulated
wheeze
clamp
tackle
prowls
fad

Discussion Questions

1. Why do you think Mr. Fridley helps Leigh stay out of trouble? Why does Mr. Fridley's concern surprise Leigh? *(Answers will vary. It seems that Mr. Fridley helps Leigh stay out of trouble because he believes Leigh is a genuinely nice boy. He realizes Leigh is going through a difficult time and any trouble he made would be a result of his stress, not his true character. Therefore, Mr. Fridley stops Leigh from doing senseless things like ruining someone else's lunch. Leigh feels isolated in his new school and thinks no one cares about or notices him. Being ignored by his father also most likely makes Leigh feel unworthy of attention. Therefore, Leigh is surprised when Mr. Fridley shows real concern.)*

2. How does Leigh feel in the grove of butterfly trees? What might the butterflies symbolize? *(Leigh is delighted and amazed by the butterflies' seeming invisibility and also by their beautiful appearance once the Sun shines on them, illuminating their bright colors. Answers will vary, but the butterflies may symbolize Leigh. The butterflies' "transformation" from invisible to proud and stunning might represent Leigh's trajectory in life. Like the butterflies, Leigh hopes to go from nearly invisible to noticed and appreciated by others.)*

3. Why is Leigh angered by his father's apology note? *(Answers will vary. The note, which was written on a napkin, seems to have been dashed off quickly. Leigh seems insulted that his father didn't take the time to write him a real letter, and he is further angered by his father including money as an apology for losing Bandit. Mostly, Leigh seems frustrated that he doesn't understand his father, though Leigh's mother explains that his father was never good at expressing himself.)*

4. Mr. Henshaw tells Leigh that "a character in a story should solve a problem or change in some way" (p. 91). Do you think the author of *Dear Mr. Henshaw* used this strategy when writing the book? *(Answers will vary, but most students will probably agree that Leigh solves several problems and changes gradually in the book. Leigh solves simpler problems, such as keeping his lunch safe and finding things to do before school. But Leigh also must contend with a much larger problem: how to cope with his parents' divorce and his new life in Pacific Grove. Over the course of the book, Leigh forgives his father, becomes more honest with his mother, adopts a more positive attitude at school, and makes a few friends.)*

5. How does Leigh make a lunchbox alarm? What does this indicate about Leigh? *(Leigh researches batteries and electricity to find out what he would need for an alarm. Then, he goes to a hardware store for supplies [and receives advice from a friendly clerk]. After fiddling with the alarm, Leigh improvises several times and creates a functioning alarm system. Answers will vary, but students will likely agree that Leigh's actions demonstrate that he is intelligent, resourceful, independent, and determined.)*

6. What happens the first day Leigh brings his alarm-rigged lunchbox to school? Why is Leigh still bothered, considering his alarm was successful? *(The lunch thief does not strike, and Leigh is forced to trigger his alarm in order to access his lunch. When the principal, teachers, and other students marvel at his invention, Leigh feels "like some sort of hero" [p. 102]. He is surprised to learn other students have had lunches stolen, and he feels happy to be noticed by others for once. Although he enjoys the attention, Leigh is still bothered because he failed to catch the lunch thief.)*

7. Why is Leigh ultimately glad he does not know the lunch thief's identity? How does Leigh's reasoning reflect his maturation over the course of the book? *(Leigh reasons that catching the thief would have only gotten him/her into trouble. He feels sympathetic toward the thief and considers that the thief could have been "just somebody whose mother packed bad lunches [or] had to pack his own lunches and there was never anything good in the house" [pp. 103–104]. Leigh also points out that whoever the thief is, Leigh has to attend school with that person. Answers will vary, but Leigh's appreciation for others' difficult situations has grown considerably over the course of the book. His thought process reflects that he has become a more thoughtful, considerate person.)*

8. How does Leigh's phone conversation with his father show that Leigh has forgiven him? *(Leigh bravely broaches the topic of Bandit and talks to his father normally. He confesses that he still misses his father, and the two end the conversation with their customary goodbyes. As a whole, the conversation demonstrates Leigh's new level of maturity and acceptance of his situation. He is able to speak to his father calmly and honestly, without becoming angry.)*

9. **Prediction:** What will Leigh submit as his Young Writers' Yearbook entry?

Supplementary Activities

1. Research: Find information about butterfly gardens. Create a visual aid explaining how to cultivate a successful butterfly garden, including what types of plants to include and where to place the garden. Present your information to the class.

2. Science: Create a simple burglar alarm using the instructions at http://www.capstonekids.com/make-stuff/projects/burglar-alarm.html (active at time of publication).

Tuesday, March 20–Saturday, March 31

Leigh submits a description of a day spent with his father for the Young Writers' Yearbook. Leigh and Barry continue spending time together, and Barry comes to Leigh's house for dinner. When Leigh's description receives an "Honorable Mention" in the Young Writers' Yearbook, Leigh is disappointed that he won't be meeting a famous author. However, through a twist of fate, Leigh gets to meet the famous author, Angela Badger, who compliments his work. Leigh's father visits unexpectedly and surprises Leigh by bringing Bandit. After Leigh's mother gently refuses Leigh's father's attempt to restart their relationship, Leigh bids his father goodbye with mixed feelings.

Discussion Questions

1. How does having Barry as a friend affect Leigh's life? *(Answers will vary, but students will most likely agree that Leigh feels much less lonely now that he is friends with Barry. Leigh also learns he is lucky in ways he never considered—lucky to have peace and quiet when he needs it, lucky to have privacy, etc. Barry helps Leigh feel like a regular kid, and visiting Barry's house exposes Leigh to another household and way of life.)*

Vocabulary
skillful
casserole
disconnect
honorable
submitted
plaid
reserved
plunk
rejected
shabby
personally

2. Why do you think Leigh asks his mother if she thinks his father will ever remarry? *(Answers will vary. Leigh obviously wishes that his parents will get back together, and he sees no logical reason why they should be apart. Leigh may also be gauging his mother's reaction so he can judge whether she still loves his father. He may also be worried that his father will "marry the pizza boy and his mother" [p. 103] and forget about Leigh as a result.)*

3. Why does Leigh have mixed feelings about receiving an "Honorable Mention" in the Young Writers' Yearbook? *(Leigh is disappointed that he didn't win first, second, third, or fourth prize and also that he won't get to meet a famous author. However, Leigh cannot deny that he feels proud to have his writing acknowledged and see his name in print.)*

4. Why is Leigh surprised that Angela Badger comments on his work? How do her comments affect Leigh? *(Leigh and his classmates were not aware that Angela Badger would have read their work. Leigh is also surprised that she remembers the full title and specific parts of his work, since, technically, his story didn't win any prizes. Perhaps Leigh predicted that Angela Badger would only like stories with subject matter similar to her own writing. Leigh is encouraged by the author's comments and vows to continue writing.)*

5. Why is Leigh's reunion with his father slightly awkward? Why are the silences during Leigh's father's visit significant? *(Answers will vary. Initially, Leigh is overcome with excitement and speeds toward his father. However, it seems like each remembers the current circumstances simultaneously. When they finally speak, it seems the important, more meaningful things are boiling beneath the surface of their casual exchange. Perhaps Leigh and his father each have so much to say that they are unable to express themselves fully. It is possible that perhaps neither wants to make the inevitable separation more difficult than it already will be. The silences during Leigh's father's visit represent things left unsaid, such as tension, sadness, and longing for a vanished way of life.)*

6. What might Leigh have learned from his parents' conversation over coffee? *(Answers will vary but might include that Leigh's parents still love each other, that Leigh's mother initiated the divorce [and had numerous reasons for doing so], and that Leigh's mother will not reconsider the divorce.)*

7. Why might Leigh's father want his son to keep Bandit? Why does Leigh insist his father keep the dog? *(Answers will vary. Leigh's father knows Leigh has a strong attachment to the dog, whom Leigh views as an ally—another "innocent victim" of the divorce. Perhaps Leigh's father would also rather not have the responsibility of caring for the dog, since life on the road can be unpredictable. Leigh honestly feels that Bandit would be happier with an exciting life of travel. He also worries about his father getting lonely. On a deeper level, perhaps Leigh wants to ensure that his father has a constant reminder of the Bottses' life as a family. He may figure that, with Bandit around, his father won't be able to forget Leigh and his mother.)*

8. What do you think Leigh's dad means when he says, "…I'll try not to let you down" (p. 134)? *(Answers will vary. Students should discuss the different ways Leigh has felt "let down" by his father in the book, which might include: [1] the divorce in general [2] his father not calling when he promises he will [3] his father "replacing" Leigh and his mom with another boy and his mother [4] his father losing Bandit [5] his father trying to apologize by sending Leigh money [6] his father's inability to change his ways.)*

9. Why does Leigh have mixed feelings at the end of the book? *(Answers will vary. Leigh has finally accepted his parents' divorce as final, so although he has closure, he mourns the absence of a parent. Leigh is glad that his father missed him and his mother, but he also worries about the loneliness of his father's profession. And although Leigh appreciates his father's visit, he has also concluded that he cannot depend on his father. For Leigh, all of these realizations are bittersweet.)*

Supplementary Activities

1. Art/Writing: Use the Postcard graphics on page 23 of this guide to design and write a postcard from Mr. Henshaw to Leigh in response to Leigh's writing accomplishment. On the front of the postcard, draw a detailed picture. On the back of the postcard, write a short note.

2. Poetry: Write a poem about a conflict Leigh experiences in the book.

Post-reading Discussion Questions

1. Why do you think the author chose to tell the story via Leigh's letters and diary entries? *(Answers will vary, but Leigh's transparency makes his character seem honest and unfiltered. The fact that readers are viewing Leigh's personal journal entries creates an intimate bond between readers and the character. Perhaps the author also wanted readers to empathize by experiencing the traumatic event Leigh is contending with—his parents' divorce—through a child's eyes.)*

2. Why do you think Leigh always describes the meals he and his mom eat? *(Answers will vary. Perhaps Leigh is trying to improve his writing skills by providing details and very specific descriptions. Leigh may also be trying to communicate that he and his mother live very simply on meager means. His descriptions of the meals ["chili out of a can" {p. 49}, "frozen chicken pies" {p. 51}, "beans and franks" {p. 111}] also reinforce that Leigh's mother is busy, with very little time to spend at home cooking more elaborate meals.)*

3. How does the author develop the "unseen" character, Mr. Henshaw, in the book? Is this character development effective? Why or why not? *(Through Leigh, the author describes Mr. Henshaw's stories and writing, giving the reader an idea of his style and tone. The reader also learns much about Mr. Henshaw from Leigh's responses to the author—responses in which Leigh mentions the advice and questions Mr. Henshaw offered. The reader also learns Angela Badger's opinion of Mr. Henshaw, whom she describes as "a very nice young man with a wicked twinkle in his eye" [p. 121]. Using all of these devices, the author indirectly builds an image and personality for Mr. Henshaw. Answers will vary, but students should consider how well they feel they know Mr. Henshaw at the end of the book to judge whether or not this character development was effective.)*

4. Why do you think the author titled the book *Dear Mr. Henshaw*? *(Answers will vary. Not only is every letter [and nearly every diary entry] begun with these words, but they become like a mantra to Leigh. Writing "Dear Mr. Henshaw" makes Leigh's thoughts and feelings flow freely. At the end of the book, Mr. Henshaw has become "dear" to Leigh, and the reader is led to believe that Leigh has become a favorite of Mr. Henshaw. The title seems to be paying tribute to Mr. Henshaw as part of the reason Leigh succeeds with his writing and his new life.)*

5. What minor problems does Leigh experience in the book? How do these smaller problems help Leigh deal with larger ones? *(Answers will vary but might include Leigh's lunch being stolen, Bandit getting lost, or Leigh's "writer's block" before the writing contest. Solving each small problem helps Leigh address a larger problem. For example, developing his lunchbox alarm helps Leigh gain popularity and feel more accepted at his school in Pacific Grove. The alarm also helps Leigh bond with Mr. Fridley, who gives Leigh sound advice about his life. Bandit getting lost [and later found] helps Leigh and his father sort out their relationship. Leigh's writer's block causes him to attempt multiple stories but ultimately write to Mr. Henshaw for advice. As a result, Leigh writes something he is proud of and learns much about himself and his talents as a writer.)*

6. What is the major conflict in the book? Do you think this conflict is resolved? Why or why not? *(The major conflict revolves around Leigh's inability to accept his new life and surroundings in Pacific Grove. Leigh still dreams about living in Bakersfield with his parents and, for a large portion of the book, has an extremely negative attitude about his life in Pacific Grove. Answers will vary, but most students will probably agree that the conflict has been resolved by the end of the book. Leigh has adopted a more positive attitude, made friends, and accepted his parents' divorce as final. He is making an honest effort to build a life in Pacific Grove with his mother. He has also come to accept that his father will never be dependable, although he is not a bad man.)*

7. Which conflicts in the book were left unresolved? Why do you think the author chose to leave these conflicts open-ended? *(Answers will vary but might include that Leigh never identified the lunchbox thief or that Leigh and his father never reached a clear understanding about their relationship. After Leigh builds his lunchbox alarm, he realizes he doesn't want to know who the thief is. Perhaps the author left this conflict open-ended to demonstrate how Leigh has grown from an angry, bitter boy into a thoughtful, more intelligent young man. As for Leigh's relationship with his father, the author most likely wanted to communicate that relationships are complicated; they take time to mend and are constantly changing.)*

8. How is Mr. Fridley important to the story's plot? *(Answers will vary, but Mr. Fridley helps Leigh in various ways. In an early letter to Mr. Henshaw, Leigh cites Mr. Fridley as his favorite person at school. Mr. Fridley also invites Leigh to help him raise the flag in the morning, eliminating the need for Leigh to stall on his way to school. It is also Mr. Fridley who gives Leigh the idea for his lunchbox alarm. Mr. Fridley sympathizes with Leigh's home situation but reminds him to consider that others have hardships, too. He encourages Leigh to adopt a positive attitude to help his life improve and generally keeps Leigh out of trouble.)*

9. What meaning can you draw from Leigh's story about the melting wax trucker? *(Answers will vary. Some students might use the truck-driving profession as a clue that this story relates to Leigh's father. Perhaps Leigh feels that the more trips his father makes, the more the emotional distance between them increases. Just as the wax trucker melts away, Leigh's father is drifting further away from his family. Leigh may also worry that his father will waste away to nothing without his family around.)*

10. What message does the book convey about families? *(Answers will vary, but the book presents the idea of the nontraditional family, such as a family that consists of a child and divorced parents. The book clarifies that the child of divorced parents does not [and should not] have to choose one parent over the other. The plot also illuminates how children of divorced parents often blame themselves for their parents' problems. Overall, the book conveys that love is most important in any type of family.)*

11. Would you recommend this book to a friend? Why or why not? *(Answers will vary.)*

Post-reading Extension Activities

Writing

1. Research the contact information for an author you admire. Create a list of questions similar to those Leigh asks Mr. Henshaw, and mail or e-mail them to your author (or his/her representative, fan club, etc.). Share any responses you receive with the class.

2. Write a short essay discussing the difficulties and dangers Leigh's father might face by allowing Bandit to travel with him.

3. Write an acrostic poem using one of the following names/words: Leigh, Bandit, thief, lunchbox.

4. Study the illustrations included in the book. Then, brainstorm a title or short description for each illustration. For example, the illustration on pages 126–127 might be titled "Close But Far Apart."

5. Write a short story about Leigh's dog titled "Bandit's Cross-Country Travels."

Science

6. Think of a problem you face on a regular basis. Then, brainstorm inventions that could help you solve that problem. Sketch a model of your invention, and present your idea to the class.

Art

7. Design and draw an alternate cover for the book using information from Leigh's letters and journal entries.

8. Create two sketches—one of Leigh's father's home in Bakersfield and one of Leigh and his mother's garden cottage in Pacific Grove.

Drama

9. Imagine that Barry was caught triggering Leigh's alarm and was therefore thought to be the lunchbox thief. Stage a courtroom scene in your classroom, and conduct Barry's trial.

Research

10. Locate different geographical points mentioned in the book on a map of the United States. Then, research one general region or city (e.g., California's Great Central Valley, the Sierra Mountains, Albuquerque, Alaska, etc.), and write a brief report with your findings.

Assessment for *Dear Mr. Henshaw*

Assessment is an ongoing process. The following ten items can be completed during study of the book. Once finished, the student and teacher will check the work. Points may be added to indicate the level of understanding.

Name _____ Date _____

Student	Teacher	
_____	_____	1. Describe how Leigh's understanding of his parents changes from the beginning to the end of the book.
_____	_____	2. Complete the Making Decisions chart on page 24 of this guide.
_____	_____	3. In an essay, explore the role Bandit plays in Leigh's strained relationship with his father.
_____	_____	4. Complete the Story Map on page 25 of this guide.
_____	_____	5. In one to two paragraphs, describe how visiting the butterfly garden helped Leigh cope with the changes in his life.
_____	_____	6. In a one-page essay, discuss whether you think the book had a happy ending.
_____	_____	7. Complete the Feelings chart on page 26 of this guide.
_____	_____	8. At the beginning of sixth grade, Leigh describes himself as "plain" and "medium." Brainstorm three adjectives that Leigh might use to describe himself at the end of the school year. Then, explain why you think Leigh's self-image changed.
_____	_____	9. Using the Venn Diagram on page 27 of this guide, compare and contrast Leigh and Barry.
_____	_____	10. Correct any quizzes or tests taken over the book.

Attribute Web

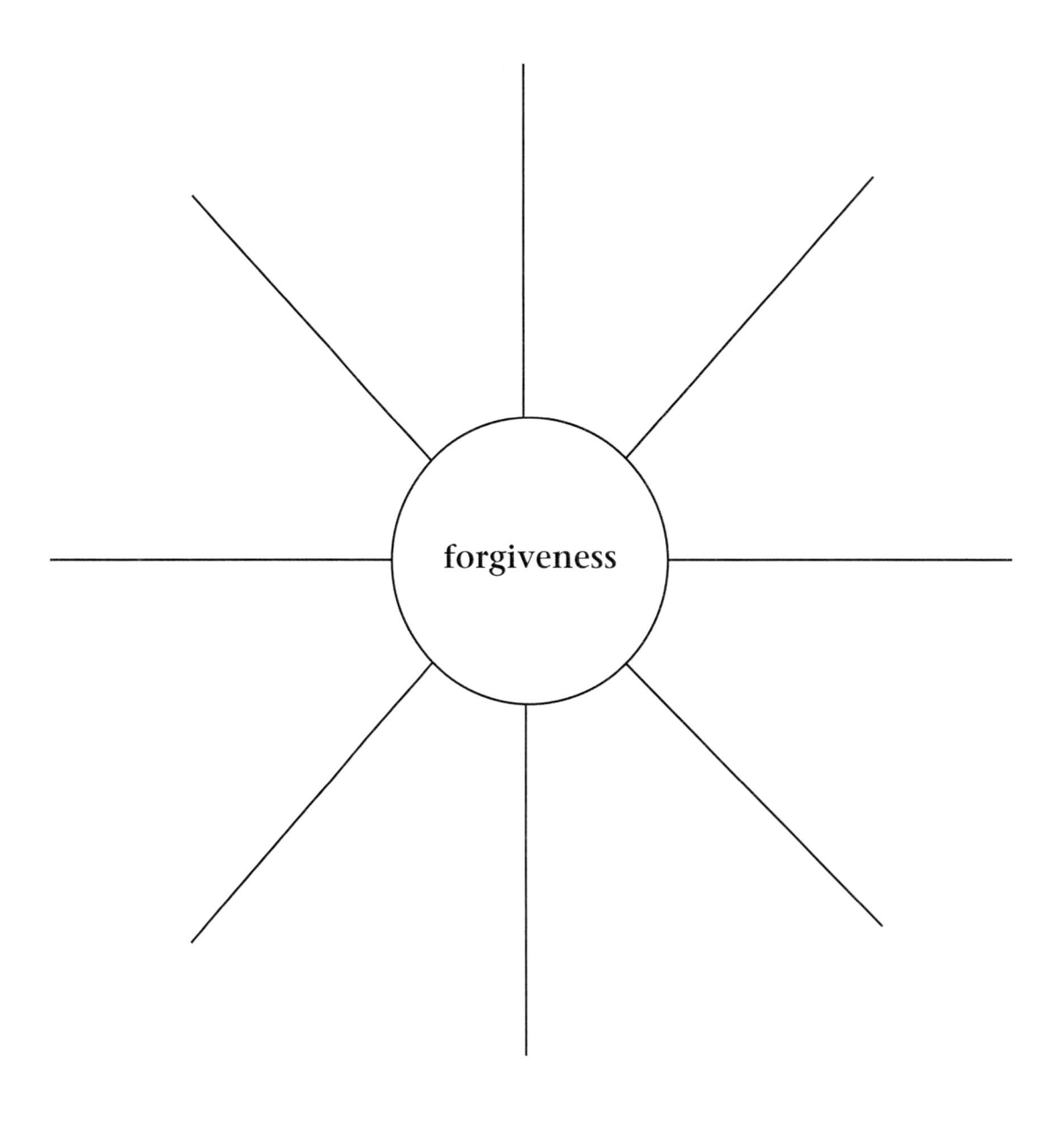

forgiveness

Character Web

Directions: Complete the attribute web below by filling in information specific to Leigh.

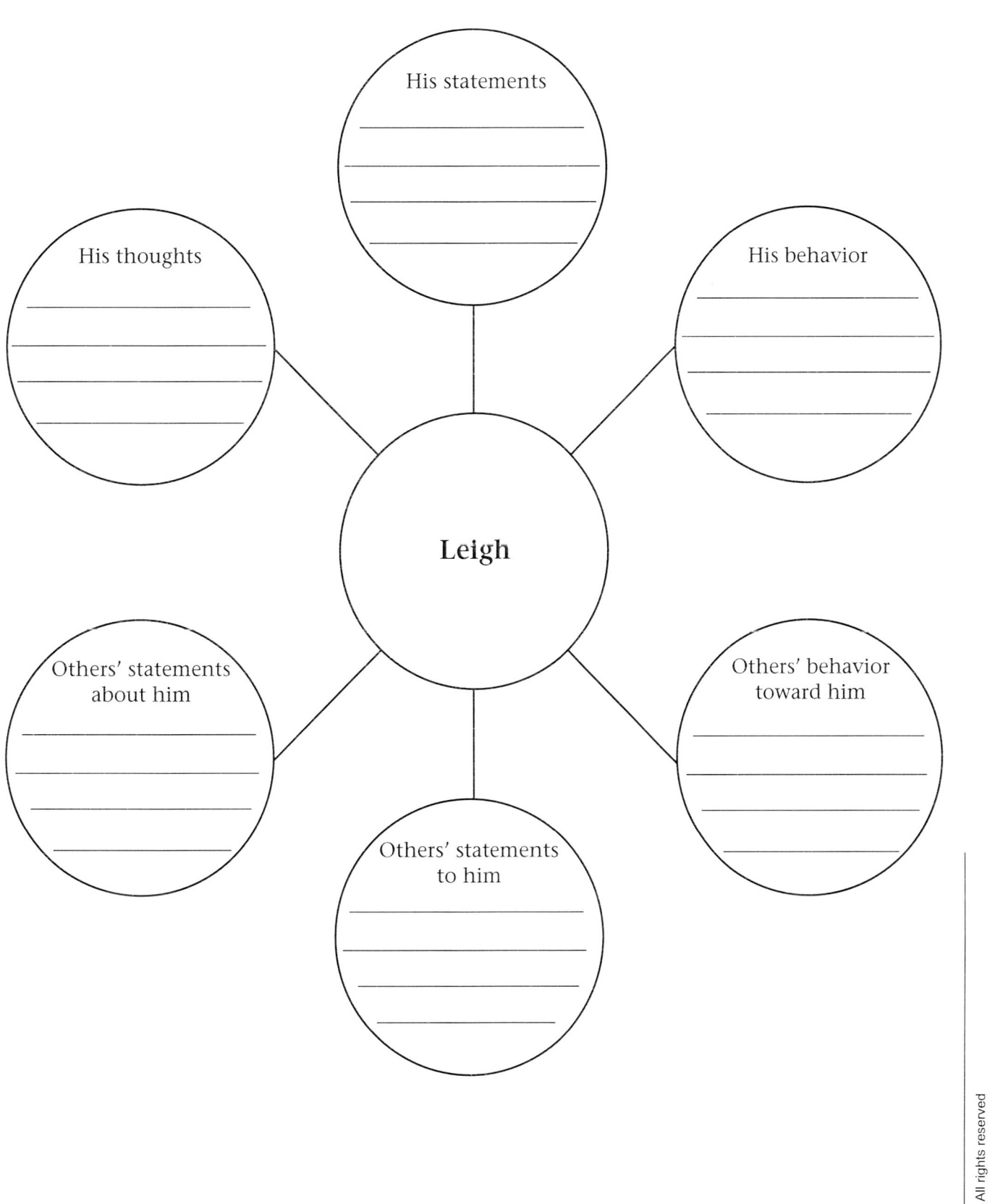

- His statements
- His thoughts
- His behavior
- Others' statements about him
- Others' statements to him
- Others' behavior toward him

Leigh

Cause/Effect Chart

Directions: Make a flow chart to show decisions a character made, the decisions s/he could have made, and the result(s) of each. (Use your imagination to speculate on the results of decisions the character could have made.)

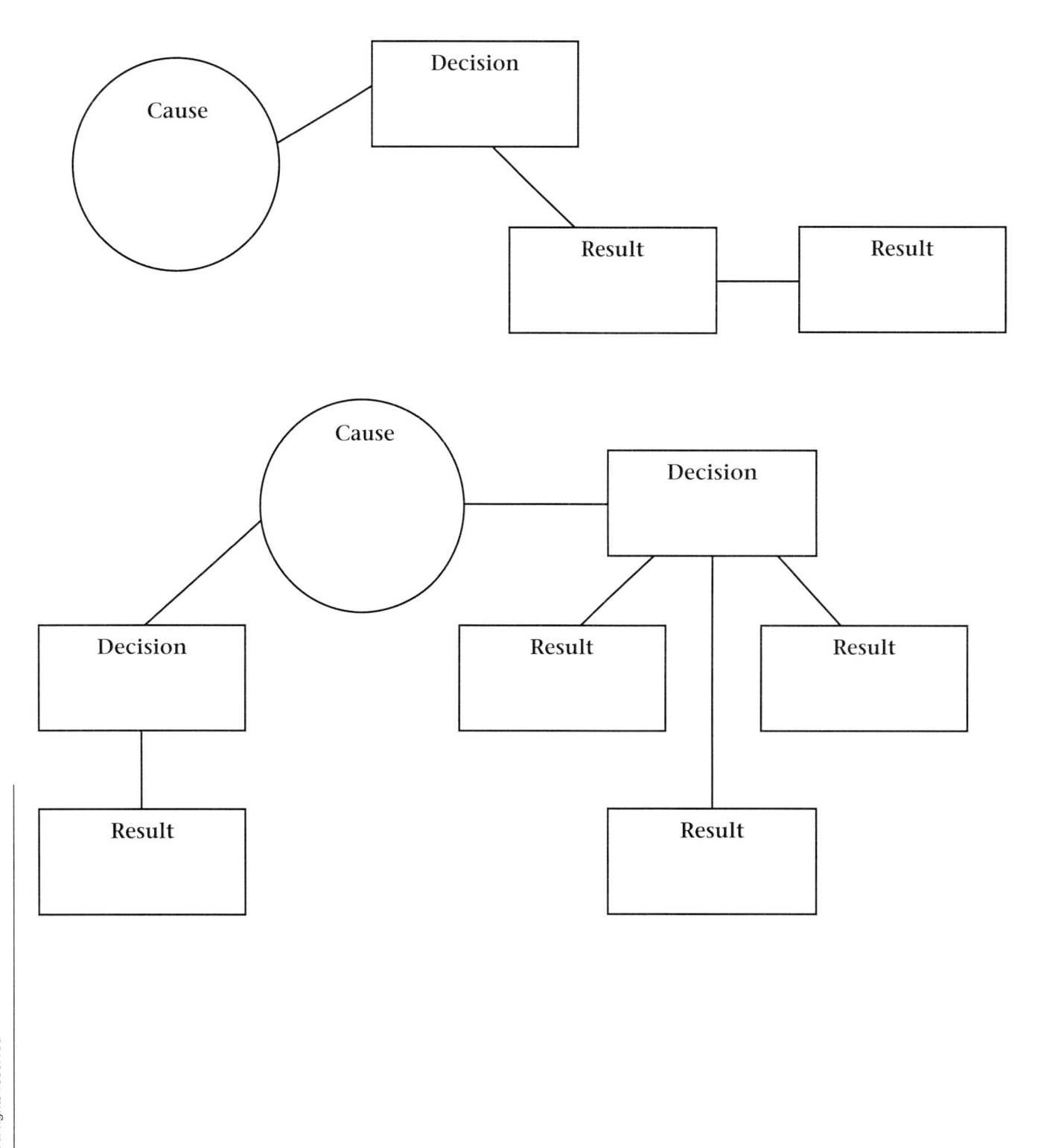

Postcard

Front

Back

Making Decisions

Directions: Determine three to seven possible solutions to the problem you write below.

    (a) State each solution in a short sentence.

    (b) Design three to five "criteria" (questions you can ask to measure how good a particular choice may be).

    (c) Rate the criteria for each solution: 1 = yes; 2 = maybe; 3 = no.

Problem: _____

Solutions ↓	Criteria				
1.					
2.					
3.					
4.					
5.					
6.					
7.					

Story Map

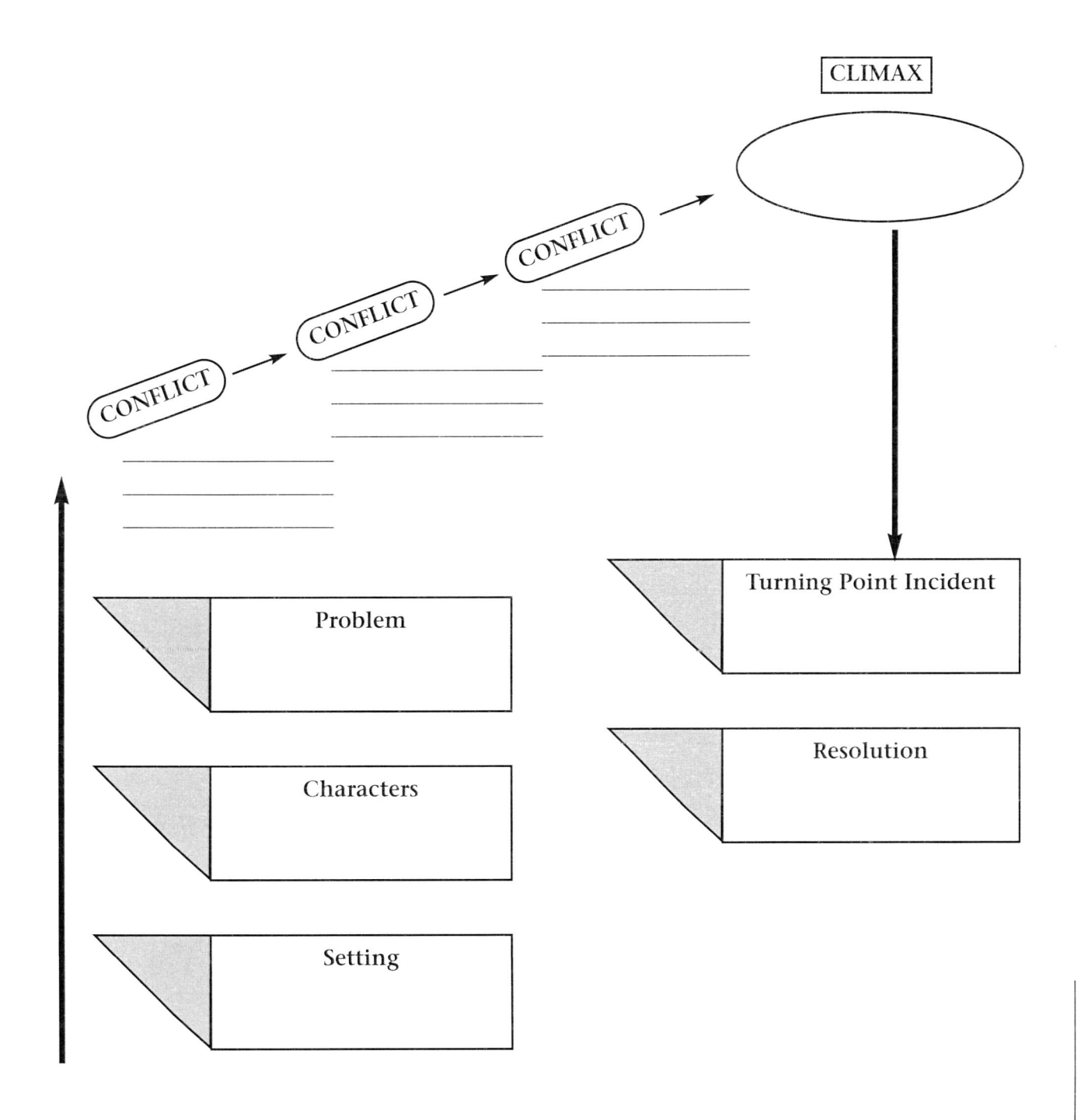

CLIMAX

CONFLICT → CONFLICT → CONFLICT →

Problem

Characters

Setting

Turning Point Incident

Resolution

Feelings

Directions: Choose a character from the book, and complete the chart below.

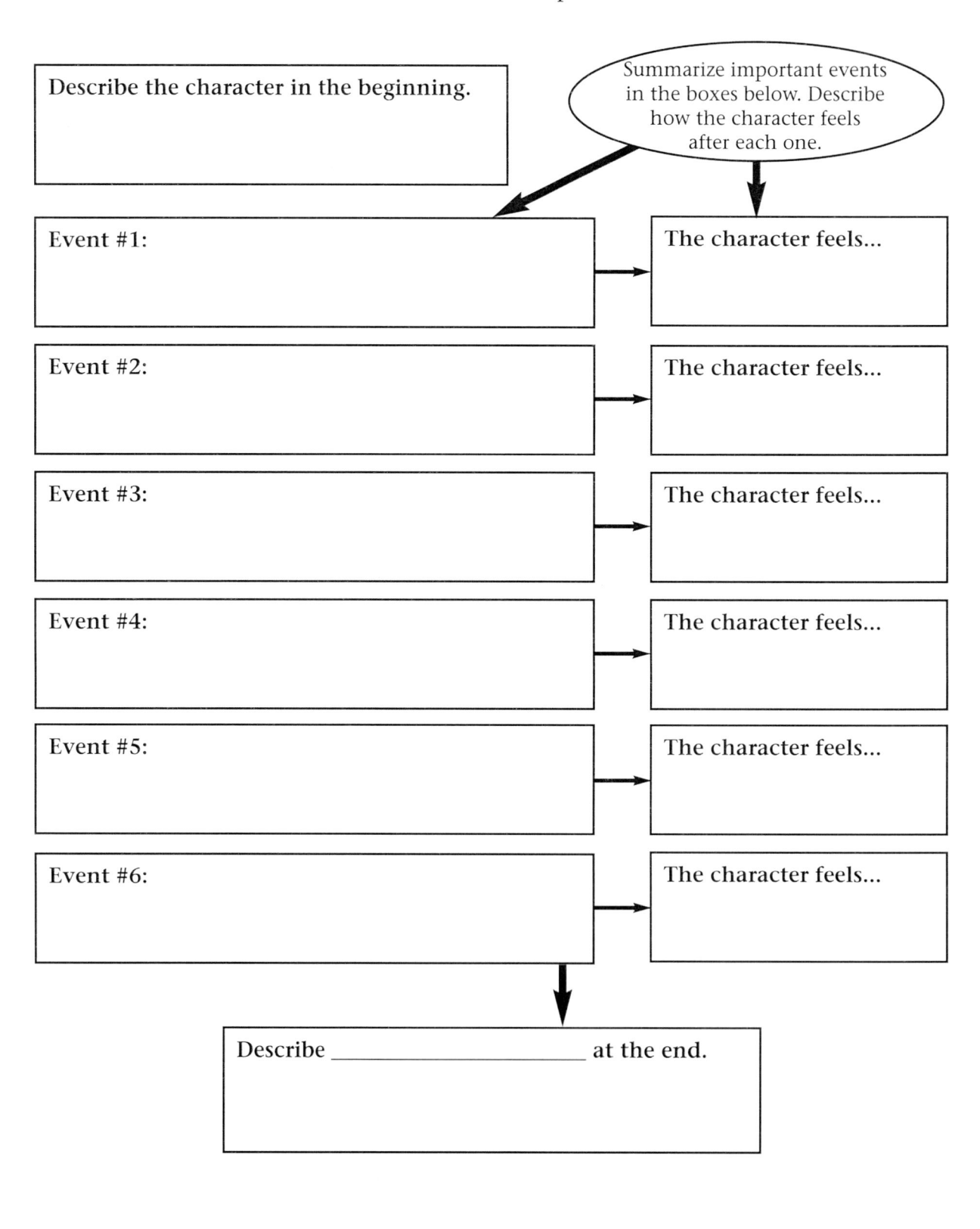

Describe the character in the beginning.

Summarize important events in the boxes below. Describe how the character feels after each one.

Event #1:	→	The character feels...
Event #2:	→	The character feels...
Event #3:	→	The character feels...
Event #4:	→	The character feels...
Event #5:	→	The character feels...
Event #6:	→	The character feels...

Describe _____ at the end.

Venn Diagram

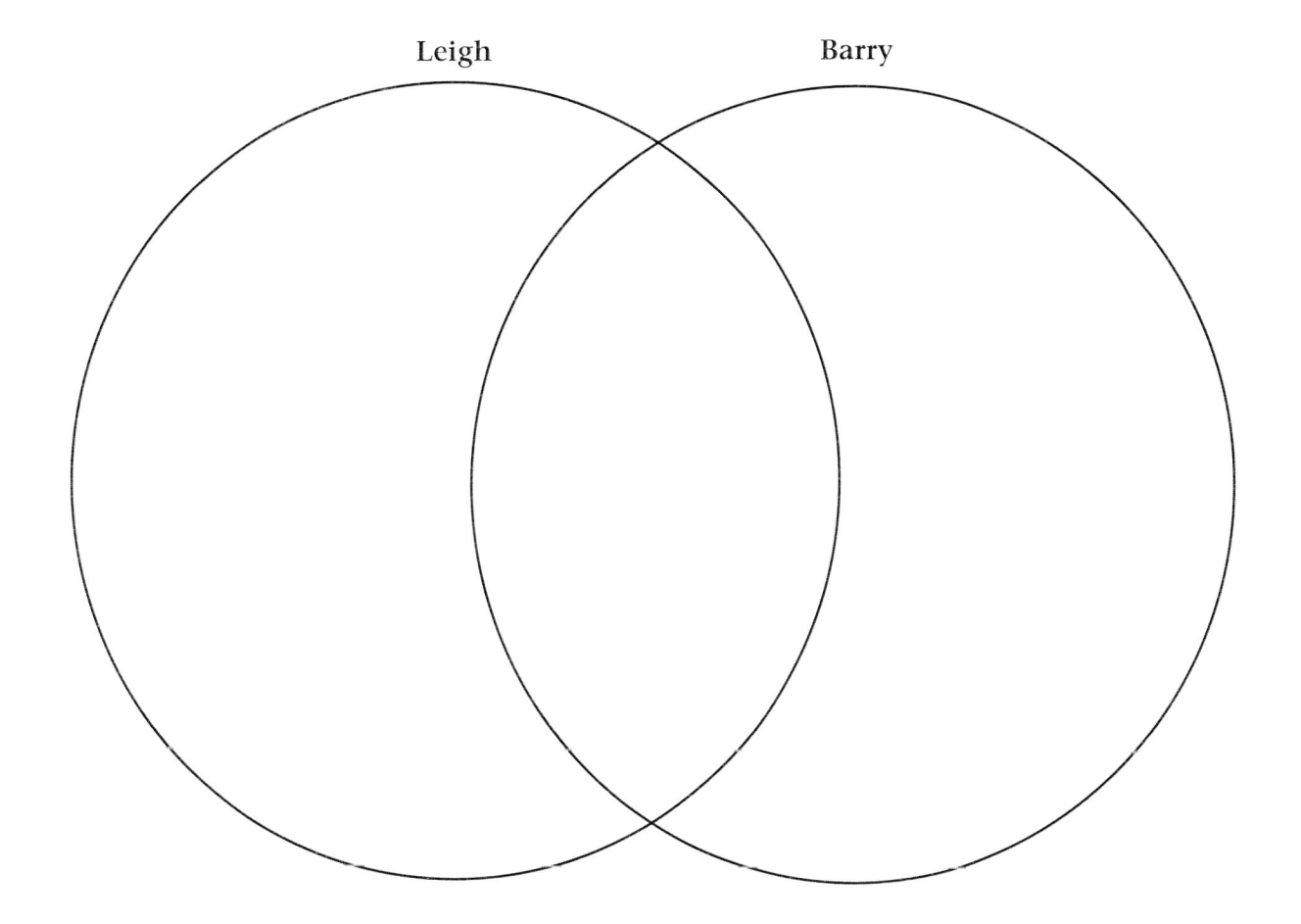

Leigh   Barry

Linking Novel Units® Lessons to National and State Reading Assessments

During the past several years, an increasing number of students have faced some form of state-mandated competency testing in reading. Many states now administer state-developed assessments to measure the skills and knowledge emphasized in their particular reading curriculum. The discussion questions and post-reading questions in this Novel Units® Teacher Guide make excellent open-ended comprehension questions and may be used throughout the daily lessons as practice activities. The rubric below provides important information for evaluating responses to open-ended comprehension questions. Teachers may also use scoring rubrics provided for their own state's competency test.

Please note: The Novel Units® Student Packet contains optional open-ended questions in a format similar to many national and state reading assessments.

Scoring Rubric for Open-Ended Items

3-Exemplary
- Thorough, complete ideas/information
- Clear organization throughout
- Logical reasoning/conclusions
- Thorough understanding of reading task
- Accurate, complete response

2-Sufficient
- Many relevant ideas/pieces of information
- Clear organization throughout most of response
- Minor problems in logical reasoning/conclusions
- General understanding of reading task
- Generally accurate and complete response

1-Partially Sufficient
- Minimally relevant ideas/information
- Obvious gaps in organization
- Obvious problems in logical reasoning/conclusions
- Minimal understanding of reading task
- Inaccuracies/incomplete response

0-Insufficient
- Irrelevant ideas/information
- No coherent organization
- Major problems in logical reasoning/conclusions
- Little or no understanding of reading task
- Generally inaccurate/incomplete response